Carla and the
Christmas Cornbread

To my mom, Audrey Hall, who always encouraged my
creativity, and to my granny, Freddie Mai Glover,
who told me that it was my job to be happy
—Carla Hall

To my mother, Audrey Atherley, for always
supporting my dream
—Cherise Harris

SIMON & SCHUSTER BOOKS FOR YOUNG READERS
An imprint of Simon & Schuster Children's Publishing Division
1230 Avenue of the Americas, New York, New York 10020
Text © 2021 by Carla Hall
Illustration © 2021 by Cherise Harris
Book design by Krista Vossen © 2021 by Simon & Schuster, Inc.
All rights reserved, including the right of reproduction in whole or in part in any form.
SIMON & SCHUSTER BOOKS FOR YOUNG READERS and related marks are trademarks of Simon & Schuster, Inc.
For information about special discounts for bulk purchases, please contact Simon & Schuster Special Sales at 1-866-506-1949
or business@simonandschuster.com.
The Simon & Schuster Speakers Bureau can bring authors to your live event. For more information or to book an event,
contact the Simon & Schuster Speakers Bureau at 1-866-248-3049 or visit our website at www.simonspeakers.com.
The text for this book was set in New Century Schoolbook.
The illustrations for this book were rendered in acrylic inks and digitally.
Manufactured in China
0821 SCP
First Edition
2 4 6 8 10 9 7 5 3 1
Library of Congress Cataloging-in-Publication Data
Names: Hall, Carla, author. | Harris, Cherise, illustrator.
Title: Carla and the Christmas Cornbread / Carla Hall ; illustrated by Cherise Harris.
Description: First edition. | New York : Simon & Schuster Books for Young Readers, [2021] | Audience: Ages 4–8. | Audience:
Grades K–1. | Summary: When Carla accidentally ruins a Christmas surprise for Santa, she must find a way to make things
right again. Includes a recipe for cornbread.
Identifiers: LCCN 2020039875 (print) | LCCN 2020039876 (ebook) |
ISBN 9781534494695 (hardcover) | ISBN 9781534494701 (ebook)
Subjects: CYAC: Christmas—Fiction. | Cornbread—Fiction. | Grandparents—Fiction.
Classification: LCC PZ7.1.H265 Car 2021 (print) | LCC PZ7.1.H265 (ebook) | DDC [E]—dc23
LC record available at https://lccn.loc.gov/2020039875
LC ebook record available at https://lccn.loc.gov/2020039876

Carla and the Christmas Cornbread

by Carla Hall
with Kristen Hartke

Illustrations by
Cherise
Harris

A Denene Millner Book
Simon & Schuster Books for Young Readers
New York London Toronto Sydney New Delhi

It's Christmas Eve, one of my favorite days of the year. That's when Mama, my sister, Kim, and I go to Granny's house to celebrate the best holiday ever: Christmas!

Every year I pack my holiday pajamas and my trusty sidekick, Bubba.

And every year I ride in the back seat, which is always piled high, high, high with Christmas presents.

The best part of the ride is watching the lights twinkle on the houses as we whiz by.

When I see the sign that says it's twenty miles to Lebanon,
I know we are almost at Granny's house.
Granny makes the best cornbread in the whole wide world.
Cornbread is my favorite.

Kim fiddles with the radio and finds a station playing the Jackson 5.
"Santa Claus is coming to town!" we all sing along.
Almost there!

Granny is looking out of the kitchen window when we pull into the driveway.

"Granny, is the cornbread ready yet?" I shout.

"Well, Merry Christmas to you, too, Carla. And Bubba."

"Merry Christmas, Granny," I say. "Is the cornbread ready yet?"

"Now that you're here, I can start baking it," she says.

Granny pulls the cast-iron skillet out of the heated oven and pours cornbread batter into it.

Hiss! Pop! The batter crackles as it hits the hot pan. Little bubbles dance around the edges.